SOME GIRLS BIND

RORY JAMES

An imprint of Enslow Publishing

WEST **44** BOOKS™

Please visit our website, www.west44books.com. For a free color catalog of all our high-quality books, call toll free 1-800-542-2595 or fax 1-877-542-2596.

Cataloging-in-Publication Data

Names: James, Rory.
Title: Some girls bind / Rory James.
Description: New York : West 44, 2019. | Series: West 44 YA verse
Identifiers: ISBN 9781538382530 (pbk.) | ISBN 9781538382547 (library bound) | ISBN 9781538383278 (ebook)
Subjects: LCSH: Children's poetry, American. | Children's poetry, English. | English poetry.
Classification: LCC PS586.3 S664 2019 | DDC 811'.60809282--dc23

First Edition
Published in 2019 by
Enslow Publishing LLC
101 West 23rd Street, Suite #240
New York, NY 10011

Copyright © 2019 Enslow Publishing LLC

Editor: Caitie McAneney
Designer: Sam DeMartin

Printed in the United States of America

CPSIA compliance information: Batch #CS18W44: For further information contact Enslow Publishing LLC, New York, New York at 1-800-542-2595.

EVERYONE HAS A SECRET IN HIGH SCHOOL

At least, that's what
my older brother, Steve, says.

Some girls date
    "bad boys."
    Sneak out their windows.
    Run off on motorcycles
    with dropouts.
    ("You know," he shrugs.
    "Like in the movies.")

Some girls ask:
    "Hey Mom, Dad,
    can I have some friends
    over to watch Disney movies?"
    Mickey and Minnie are harmless.
    But they always wear gloves.
    Maybe it's so they don't
    leave fingerprints on
    their parents' wine bottles.

Some girls play
    spin the bottle,
    around and around it goes.
    But I don't know.
    I've never met anyone
    who has actually played.

My friends see movies
and eat ice cream.
　　　And, according to my mother,
　　　have "teenage" problems.

(Three years
into my teens,
and not even I
know what she
means by this.)

I'm pretty sure
　　　my parents
　　　would never believe
　　　that I was one of
　　　"those girls."

Would never think
that I have a secret.

　　　(I'm not, I do).

My friends have secrets too,
but not like the ones
found in the feel-good
section of Netflix:

    Levi's gay.
        (He and Evan Holmes
        just started dating.
        But neither has told his parents.)
    And

    Nora's dad drinks too much.
        (She puts her brothers
        to bed every night.)
    And

    Eric wants to drop out of swimming.
        (But doesn't
        because of scholarships.)
    And

    I think Jason and Callie
    have secrets too, but
        we all hang out
        and don't talk about them.

Instead,
we pile into Eric's van
and drive to the park.

Climb down
onto the rocks
by the canal.
Off of the trails where

our parents
brought us for
Sunday cookouts.
Days with
picture-perfect
picnic baskets and
family Frisbee matches.

We talk about
our classmates and
our teachers.
Complain about
homework, tests,
and quizzes.

We talk about
everything except
the feeling of keeping secrets.
But we do keep them here,
in this place.

Levi was the first to share his.

Coming out to us was
a rite of passage
scarier than becoming a man.
Nora rose first to hug him,
maybe remembering
the way they danced
at his bar mitzvah.
He dropped the rock
he'd been holding. The one
he meant to skip.
We all picked up his secret.

One by one,
we each come
to the canal.

Pick a normal weekend outing.

Hold court.
Call a meeting.
All of those adult terms
we'd heard our
parents talk about.
To say to the water what scared us most.
To watch our reflections
instead of meeting friends' eyes.

We listen for secrets
and we tell our own.

All of us except
for me.

I have one, too. And
I had hoped
it would join
my brother's list of examples.
That I would be a "some girl."

But, of course,
what other teenage girl
binds her chest
because she's not sure
she's a girl?

TIES THAT BIND

I started when I was 14.
    Found a once too-big
    (now too-tight) vest.
    The buttons strained over a
    white undershirt.
    I wrapped tape around
    the shoulders of the vest,
    forming thin straps
    not exactly hidden.

No one could get too close.
    Couldn't run their fingers
    over my back.
    Notice the braless broad shoulders
    covered in the silk of a stretched vest.

Getting dressed each morning,
    I stand behind my door.
        Off to the side. So if it opens,
I am behind it. Hidden by
the Scooby-Doo blanket I use
as a closet door.
I feel its soft
fleece as
I pull one layer and
    then another over my shoulders.

I remember the first time I wore it,
    the first time I felt the ridge
    of one button
    slide into place and
    then the next.

The first time I added
    another layer
    to my already boyish style
    hiding beneath T-shirts.

My parents were
    out of town for the day.

I was free.

That day, I'd curled next to my dog,
        toyed with the idea of binding,
        of my body looking more
        like what I expected to see
        in the mirror.
        The idea grew
        and grew. The pages
        left in my summer reading
        lessened. My
        notes of quotes for the paper
        I had to write sat off to the side.

I snuck into my room for no reason.
        Asked my dog to keep this secret
        as he had all others.
        (He did.)

MY PARENTS

My mother already wondered why
      I wore white undershirts every day.
      Gave me a hard time
      when, in the store,
      I'd try to put a set in our cart.
      She'd ask, "Where did you even get this idea?"

I knew that "Dad" was not
      the right answer,
      though it was the truest.
      I watched the line
      between men and me drawn
      in permanent marker on the drive home.
      Watching the white dotted lane lines
      become a solid double yellow.

 I soon used money from my job at the library
      to buy undershirts by myself so Mom wouldn't see.

The vest on my chest would be her shame.
      The binder,
      a binding family secret. So
      I say nothing, hide everything.

I barely know how to explain it to myself.
That it's like a corset
designed to make me look
boyish.
That it seems to suit me.
That I feel more confident
with my chest flatter, unlike
any girl in my class.

(Or my school or my small town or my life.)

I don't even know if I want to be one.

My parents would think that this means
I'm gay.
But I'm not even sure
if anyone would want me.
Would want my bound chest.
Would want this secret.

Every once in a while,
    my friends will say,
            "That's gay."

    Or my parents will
    wonder,
                "Why do shows now
                    have so many queers?"
    Like it's a bad thing
    with a word they shouldn't use.

And I think,
    Would they say
    these things
    about me?

But
> binding feels so good, so right. Like a weight
> that should hold me down,
> but lifts me up.

I am confident
> but cannot be close to anyone,
> for fear they would say
> it's wrong.

They could trace the thicker straps,
> the smooth back, and unusual shape
> if I'm not careful.
> So I've given up tight shirts,
> white shirts, not enough shirts.
> Added layers.

My secret is buried in more ways than one.
But it is from this depth
that I feel like me.

DOES ANYONE ACTUALLY LIKE GYM CLASS?

Gym class comes, as it does
        in high school. And so
        I change in the big stall.
        Dart out of the cafeteria and confront

the signs.
        You know:
        the man standing tall and
        the woman standing skirted.

I look like neither.
        Long hair pulled back
        into a ponytail, baggy pants
        and a hoodie.

I'm not sure I'm either.
        When I look in the mirror,
        I don't see a girl and
        I don't see a boy. I just see
        my goofy glasses and Beatle-like hair.

This is new,
        the idea of being neither.
        Of being "genderqueer."

And yet, I don't know if this
        is what or who I am.

What does it mean?
    Am I not "Daddy's little girl"?

Do I lose status as daughter?
    Sister? Niece?
    Child? Friend?

If I am neither,
    am I nothing?

This is what I hear
    echoing in my head
    every time I change for gym,
    each time I see those signs.

It's not that I don't
        "fit in."
        There's always a "Hey, Jamie"
        in each class. A friend to sit near.
        To hate homework with or to pair up with
        for a project.

That sometimes makes it harder.
        What would they think?
        Would I be partnerless,
                powerless,
if I couldn't say whether I was a
                "girl-space-friend" or a
                "boy-space-friend?"

NORA

Nora changes
　　in the stall next to me.
　　(She's got her own
　　marks to hide.) And
　　it's nice to have class
　　together.

She always says she's sorry
　　to our friends for not
　　being around. And today
　　is no different. As we
　　stretch before gym, she says,

　　　　　　　　"Jamie, I'm sorry I wasn't
　　　　　　　　　　there on Saturday.
　　　　　　　　Connor and Colin
　　　　　　　　had soccer practice. And
　　　　　　　　then I had to make dinner.
　　　　　　　　And
　　　　　　　　do that paper I had for bio.
　　　　　　　　And
　　　　　　　　I was so tired." And

she looks brokenhearted,
　　like she's saying sorry to herself.

"Nora," I say,
      pretending to stretch.
      More focused on reaching
      for the right words than
      on touching my toes.

"It's okay. We miss you,
      but
      we know it's hard."

This is a lie, and she knows it.
How could we
understand the way her
father works each day,
drinks each night?

How could we understand
how her mother chooses
to miss every day
with her children?

How could we understand
how Nora chooses
to not miss any day
with her brothers,
even if we miss her?

Still, we have to say this.
Have to pretend that
this is not harder
than
our own struggles,
so that Nora
feels like she fits.

"God,"
Nora says,
but it's not a prayer.
(She also says
she's given up on the divine
Him/Her/Them/They.)
She finishes:

"I hate gym. It makes me
        so uncomfortable."

Nora is the most thoughtful
        person I know.
        And I know that
        she couldn't know
        (and would be *so sorry* to know)

how I feel watched.
        Looked at. Seen in the
        T-shirt the girls
        have to wear, tighter
        than the boys'.
        Too afraid
                to say, "Hey,
        can you order me the
        boys' shirt
        instead?"

It's much easier to reply
        "me too" and keep
        doing sit-ups,
        to keep going.

SOMETIMES FLANNEL IS A MASK

Mom asked me to help sort
    Steve's old clothes.

I think
    it's her way of
    getting rid
    of the ones
    she hated.

I imagine
    she'll do the same
    with mine.

I'm sure
    she dreams of me
    growing out of this
    baggy, boyish
    box.

"Can you believe
he used to wear this?"
She holds up an AC/DC shirt
with the sleeves
cut off.
It must be
almost as old as I am.

I laugh, thinking of
    my preppy
    baseball
    brother
    walking around
    with no sleeves.
    "Oh Steve."

Steve made the varsity team
        as a sophomore.
        Started halfway through
        and played second base
        in college.

My brother's a nice guy,
        studies medicine,
        will be the best doctor.
        And I think he's
        the poster child
        for athletes:
        skilled, smart, and
        sensible.

My parents don't want
        me to be Steve.
        And Steve doesn't want
        me to be Steve. But man,
        wouldn't it be easier
        if I was just like him?

Mom pulls out an old flannel shirt.
 And I remember
 teasing Steve
 for looking like
 a lumberjack.

We each took our turn:

Dad:

   "Make sure you chop
   enough wood to make it
   through winter, son!"

Mom:

   "If you're cutting trees down,
   check them for birds first.
   You don't want any nests falling!"

Me:

   "I don't think this is
   what people mean when they say,
   'log in,' Steve."

Now, though,
        I think that flannel might be
        a good look for me.

Women wear flannel. And
        men wear flannel. So
        I could, too.

Mom leaves the room, and
        I pull it out of her pile.
        I start
        a one-shirt stack
        of my own
        where she can't see.

THEY'RE SAD TO SEE ME GO, BUT SOMETIMES I HAVE TO

My parents are used to me
            disappearing on weekends.
            Bouncing between
            coffee shops.

My mother smiles,
            but she looks at me sadly
            as I drive away.
            As if I've already
            left for college.

My father says,

                        "Hey, Jamie,
                        want to go
                        to a movie
                        (or to a bookstore
                        or restaurant
                        or anywhere)?"

Both are so afraid
            to lose their daughter
            when she grows up. But

I'm afraid that
            I'll lose them
            if I tell them my secret.
            If I tell them what
            I leave home
            to think about, alone.

So, on Saturday, I am driving
        further than usual. Out
        to a place
        I've never been
        as a person
        I've never been.

Wearing my brother's flannel,
        which he wore at 14.
        Even though I'm
        almost 17,
        it's still a size
        too big,
        but

it's comfortable.

The shirt feels different. My binder
keeps me flat. My hair in my hat
makes me more boy
than boyish.

I think this
should make me feel
better, but I'm not sure
it's me.

You never know
until you try,
right?

I plop
        into a booth,
        coffee in hand.
        Putting my books,
        laptop,
        pens, notepads

        (my whole locker)

        on the table.
        Try to work
        on a paper for English,
        on questions for math,
        on this new identity.

CHANGING MY WORLD

I think that
>I've always felt
>like everyone is
>watching me. As if
>they know
>(because they must know)
>that I'm different.

So today,
>this feeling
>is stronger than ever.
>Like the man at the table
>behind me
>can see through
>my disguise.

Or the woman
>at the counter
>who has seen
>and smiled at me
>knows that I'm a girl
>pretending.

But I'm not.
        I'm not.
        I'm not pretending
        to be anything.
        I'm just trying to
        be myself.

In this shop,
        I turn images of
                myself
                        over
                                and
                                        over.

What would it be
        to be
        a boy,
                ordering a pastry,
                smiling, talking, working?

I feel like
        this should fit, but
        it doesn't. And
        the reality of
        being a girl
        doesn't either.

What if this is a test
        and the answer is
                all of the above?

What if I am always watched
        but not seen?

What if people always see
        the misfit and don't accept
        the neither?

What if I must always be
        a girl? Or a boy?
        When I'm not one
        or the other.

So I go home,
        having changed
        into my usual clothes
        in the car. And

I sit in my room,
        homework not done.
        And I know
        that I am indeed neither.
        That I was right:
        I'm genderqueer.

SIGN ON THE BINDING LINE

I write it out,
    this new identity,
    this new me,
    this new Jamie.

I watch the
    twist of the "g,"
    the twirl of the "q"
    as ink forms the word
    on the page.

This great new secret,
    the ink rightly binding,
    like a contract.

I even sign my name below.

This leads to a lot and
        a little, all at once.

I am afraid to say anything,
        even though
        nothing would change
        for those around me.

It's about me,
        but I know
        it can't be
        (it isn't)
        that simple.

And so it starts,
        this process
        of being new.

Every day, I find
        something new
        that tells me
        I must either be a
        boy or a girl:

the bathroom signs,
        clothing stores,
        "Ladies and Gentleman,"
        birthday cards,
        Christmas cards.
        Even toothbrushes
        have a binary gender—
        that is, male or female.

What about me?
        I am left out,
        and no one sees
        the problem.

Thankfully, no one questions
        when I use the women's room
        or when I buy boy's this
        and girl's that,
        a hodgepodge mix.

THERE ARE MOMENTS WHEN I WANT TO SHOUT

I don't want
    to keep
    this secret.
    It's tiring,
    and I don't
    want to be alone.

I don't want
    to tell all
    of my friends though,
    either. So what do
    I do?

Nora would be
        wonderful. Of course
        she would.

Eric's so busy with
        swimming. And
        I'm not sure
        how he'd react.

Levi, though.
        My genderqueerness
        is not the same
        as his gayness. But

he was told men only love
        women and defies it.
        And I was told
        there are only
        men and women
        and defy it.

WE'RE A SMALL GANG

When I met Levi,
    he told me that
    Levi jeans were
    only for him.

I said,
    "That's not true."
    And he paused,
    thinking.
    (As six-year-olds do.)

        "Okay. You can wear them
        if you want."

That was first grade. And
        we've moved together
        to middle and then
        high school, collecting
        friends for our
        little gang.

We're an odd mix
        of people.
        And my parents joke
        that, secretly, we rule
        the school.

Levi and I laugh about this.
        Where did
        they go
        to school if
        they think
        we're popular?

It all happened by accident:

Jason lived next door to Levi.
    And he sat with Nora
    on her first day
    as the new kid. And
    I came along with Levi.

Callie and Eric came next
    in junior high. And then
    she and Jason started dating
    last year.

Levi's been there,
　　　always. After he came out,
　　　he told me that
　　　he had a crush on
　　　my brother Steve.

And, although
　　　Steve is straighter
　　　than the pitches
　　　he throws,
　　　there's a part of me
　　　that still hopes that
　　　Levi could be
　　　my brother-in-law
　　　one day.

A COMING OUT

I text Levi a week after
        my identity becomes
        clear to me.

(I wanted to give it time
        to sink in.)

(I wanted to give myself time
        to sink in.)

"Hey."
(I text.)

"Hey, J, what's up?"
(Levi answers.)

"Can we hang out soon?"

"Yeah! I miss you."

"Okay.
I have something to tell you."

"Is everything okay?"

"Yeah, I think so."

"Wednesday?"

"After school?"

"Yes"

"Perfect."

"<3"

"<3"

I know Levi
        is the least likely
        to judge me. But
        I'm still pacing
        when he picks me up.

We go to our place,
        since it's still
        warm enough
        to hike
                down
                        to the
                                water.

"It feels like it's
        been forever since
        we were last here."
I say, looking for
        skipping stones.
        My usual habit.

            "Yeah, this year's been
                    crazy. I can't
                    remember
                    the last time
                    Eric was with us,"
            Levi says.

"I wish he'd quit the swim team."

        "Me too."

I should
start. Even Levi
seems nervous.
Instead, I ask,

"How's Evan?"

Levi smiles,
"He's really
good."

"Good."

Then silence.

"So Levi, I,
       I don't…"

Breathe, I tell myself.

"I don't think,
I know that
I'm not,
I'm not a girl."

Halfway there.

"I'm also not a boy."

So…

"I'm genderqueer."

Levi doesn't
        let me catch
        my breath
        before smiling and saying,
        "Okay, cool."

He hugs me,
        starts crying with me.
        (This is normal.)
        Says, "Congrats."
        Makes this day a celebration.

After all, he knows how to
        come out.

He does not:
      say "I knew it,"
      ask what that means,
      hate me.

He does:
      say "I'm proud of you,"
      ask how I knew,
      love me.

IT'S NICE TO FEEL NORMAL

Like this is
normal and
     okay.

Levi is set
     on making sure
     I know all of this
     to be true.

By the end of the day,
     we shout over the small,
     man-made waterfall:
     "We're here, and
     we're queer."

I tell him
    how scared I am,
    how I like this identity,
    how I don't know
    how to explain it to
        anyone else. But

with each nod,
    I hear him say,
            "I know,
                it's going to be okay."

"So what about
          pronouns?"
Levi asks this
as he weaves the car
out of the park.
          "How should I refer to you?"

I had thought
     about this.
     It's a question
     that pops up
     (according to Google).

"'She' is feminine,
        but I guess
        I'm okay
        with it."
        I pause. "But
        I think I prefer 'they.'"

"They"
        doesn't have
        a gender, so
        even though
        it means more than one,
        I like it.

                "Whatever you want, J.
                I just want you
                        to be happy."

I get out
    of the car, back
    at school, where
    I left mine to drive together.

Levi stops, promises me that
    even though
    this will be hard
        ("And it will be,
            which sucks, so I'm sorry."),
    he's there.

I hug him again,
    squeeze his hand,
    and I get out of the car.

And that's the
    first time
        I come out.

Levi doesn't tell
        Evan or
        anyone. Even though
        it'd almost
        be easier if I let him.

I get home
        from our hike, and
        my mom asks
        how it was.

"Really great.
        It's been so long
        since I've seen Levi."

She winks, I think,
        as I go into my room.
        Which
        makes me laugh.
        If only she knew.

IN THE CLOSET BUT ON THE ROAD

I start telling Levi
    everything.
    We drive
        further and further
            out on day trips.

Sometimes
    he brings Evan,
    who I loop in because
    Levi is
    my best friend, and
    Evan is important
    to him and so
    to me.

We go to Rochester
    when we can.
    Hide in this city
    just up the I-90.
    Exist in a place where
    our secrets
    don't matter.

Evan and Levi
    walk up East Avenue,
    get ice cream,
    kiss in front of
    pride flags.

"J!" Levi laughs,
       and I don't think
       I've ever
       seen him so happy.
"This restaurant has
       gender-neutral restrooms!"

He points at a little café.
       We come back once,
       twice, as often as we can.

Walking in, it feels
     the same as the shops
     back home. But

I wander back, past
     bulletin boards of LGBT+
     events and
     things I want to do.

Toward two doors that are
     the same. No little man.
     No little woman.

I get to choose.

THE THINGS I NEVER THOUGHT TO THINK ABOUT

I ask Levi
    a million questions
    about being gay or
    about gender or
    anything, really.

"Why doesn't
    genderqueer have
    a letter in 'LGBT+?'"

"Should I change my name?
    Jamie is both a boy's name
    and a girl's name though…"

"Does this mean I'm gay? A lesbian?"

Levi doesn't give me
answers. He says,

"Jamie."
He places one hand
on my shoulder.
Weaves
our fingers together.
"You have to decide
some of this for
yourself."

"Whatever you decide—
Jamie, James,
gay, straight,
whatever—
it's okay."

Sitting up
        past midnight,
        my dog at the end
        of my bed,

I do a lot
        of research.
        Find that
        genderqueer is new.

Decide to
        keep my name.
        And decide to not think
        too much
        about romance,
        not yet.

(One coming out
        at a time.)

Everyone else is asleep,
        but my world is
        changing.

I tell this to Levi,
  and he nods.
    "Sounds good."

It's simple
  and it's easy
  to think that
  I need his approval.

But
  I'm trying
  to make sure
  that I think about
  my happiness, too.

(I'm much happier
  just being able
    to talk about it.)

HITTING THE BOOKS

I've spent days
    on the floor
    of my room.
    Only getting up
    to refill my water bottle or
    pull a new book
    off of my shelf.

Now,
    I look for the
    "books of my people,"
    stories about gender,
    sexuality.

I lose myself there,
 spend hours
 with new heroes.

Even *A Midsummer Night's Dream*
 makes my list:
 Puck seems
 a little queer to me.

I pretend
 there are more
 like me
 who
 blend girl and boy,
 pink and blue, to
 make purple.

Each morning,
    I bind.
       And while Levi
           grows closer
               to me,

I still keep
       this secret
       for me alone.

It's never come up,
       even in the endless
       hours of
       driving.

I suppose
        that I still
        feel shame. Like
        I'm denying

something natural
        by tucking and
        tightening
        my chest. But

it's too
        comforting, like
        the tightness
        is a sign that
        I finally fit.

IT WOULD BE NICE

to not be
        the only "they"
        that I know,

and it seems like
        college will be
        my escape.

But that's a year away,
        and I still haven't
        said anything
        to my parents.

Talking to Levi helped.
        And sometimes I think
        that coming out can
        fix the secret. But I will
        still be alone,
        will still be the only
        "they."

It would be nice
	to find someone
	who understands

what it is

		to wear a "they/them" pin
			each day. Or

		to correct those that ignore
			this pin. Or

		to choose a restroom. Or

		to say "hey, y'all" instead of
			"hey, guys." Or

		to be tired by
			gendered things. Or

		to do so many things.

MY FAVORITE BOOKSTORE, RENEWED

I look for
> others
> online.
> People who bind.
> People who understand.
> So

when I hear of a poet
> who's like me
> (genderqueer!)
> coming to
> Buffalo,

I tell my parents
> I have to go
> for a project. And
> drive into the city.

I don't ask Levi
        or Evan or
        Nora or
        anyone
        to come—

this is for me.

My dad brought me here
        when I was younger.
        A small bookshop tucked
        into a small
        neighborhood.

He knew I'd love it.
        This little corner of the block.
        This little corner of the world.

It was small. The
        spines on shelves
        were a puzzle of other places.

I always believed
        in other universes.
        Of places and lives
        we couldn't imagine. Except
        here they were in this store,

and I could go
        to each one.

My father is
        a scientist,
        does research
        on cancer,
        comes home tired,
        often stressed.

But here, in this store,
        he told me
        stories that
        I think
        he wanted
        science to prove.

Tonight, I will
　　　see a life
　　　like the one
　　　I am scared to have.

I slip into the back,
　　　leaning right.
　　　I pass the shoulders
　　　of those taller than me.

People holding books
　　　of poetry like
　　　the one I just bought.

They are waiting calmly
　　　while, for some reason,
　　　I am nervous.

Yet at the same time I'm home
    because some of these
    people look like
    people, not just
    men and women.

That is, they look like me.
    Or, rather,
    I look like them.

Finally.

The poet is not
        loud.
        Does not write only
        on their gender.
        Is simply
        living their life.

Their hair is
        cut short,
        whisps coming out
        of the sides of their red hat.
        It matches their lipstick,

which matches
        the red of a bow tie
        around their neck.

They still look formal,
        in a dress shirt
        and suspenders, which sit
        on shoulders that

I think may hold
        some of my hopes.

They speak
　　softly, lips barely
　　touching
　　the microphone.
　　Smiling
　　　　as they read.

We all hear them though,
　　as they speak
　　on gender,
　　on genderqueerness,
　　on being looked at twice.

Yes, I am so afraid of that, too.

Maybe, one day,
　　I could speak like this.
　　Could talk about binding
　　like it's normal,
　　like it's okay.
　　Because it is.
　　(I just have to accept that.)

They sign books
　　at the end,
　　kindly greet each
　　of us, ask our names
　　and

our pronouns. So
　　I shyly say,

"Hi, Jamie.
　　That is, *I'm* Jamie, and
I use they/them."

They shake my hand,
        like they know
        what I'm going through.
        And then I remember,
        they do.

                    "It's nice to meet you, Jamie.
                        Thanks for coming."

And they wink
        as they hand
        my book back.

YOU LEARN SOMETHING NEW EVERY DAY

"That's the gay wink,"
    Levi concludes
    when I tell him.

I look at him funny
    and he continues,
    "No, I know you aren't gay.
    I'm just referring
    to the whole
    LGBT+ community.

And some people choose
    to say 'gay'
    to sum it up.

Anyway, LGBT+ humans
    tend to know
    when they're in
    good company,
    so they'll wink or nod.

It happens to
    Evan and I sometimes."

"Sure," I reply,
    like it doesn't matter,
    but it's the first time
    a stranger knows.
    And it's the first time
    a stranger still smiles at me.

The book slides
    onto my shelf
    in the way
    I wish to fit in—
    easily.

I'M NOT EVEN OUT OF BED YET

"Knock, knock, Jamie,"
    says my dad,
    pushing the door
    and coming in.

It's Saturday,
    and I'm barely awake.
    Still lying in bed,
    reading poetry.

He sits down
    on the edge
    of the mattress,
    like he always does.

"I always forget
    how bad
    your breath is
    in the morning."
He laughs. Dad humor.
    "What are you reading?"

"Just a poet
    I like."

It's the one
    from the reading.
    I haven't been
    able to leave it
    alone for more than a day.
He gestures for it,
        wants to see it.
        An innocent request.

So I hand it over.

                "This is…different."
                He's looking
                at the poet's picture,
        "This…" He pauses. "…person
                has an interesting look."

        Then he shrugs,
                "Have fun with it.
                You always find
                interesting things
                to read."
I can't read him
    though.

What does "different" mean?
    "Interesting"?
    Why did he pause before "person"?

NOT READY

"Jamie."
My mom welcomes me home
from school.
"How was your day?"

"School was fine," I reply,
    walking past her
    to my room. And
    it's true.

School's fine.
    I keep my friends
    close
    and I go to my
    nerdy club meetings,
        choir and the newspaper,
        hang out with Levi and Evan.

No one really knows,
        but someone does,
        and I know
        where to find
        others like me
        (my bookshelf).
                And, for now,
                that's good,

even if I'm dreaming
        of not hiding.

                        "I haven't seen many
                                of your friends
                                lately.
                                Just Levi.
                                        Is everything okay?"

"Oh yeah," I reply,
        but feel
        guilty right away.
        "Everything's good.
        They've just been busy."

I text Levi that night:

"Do you think that
I should tell
everyone?
Well,
our friends."

"Sort of?"

"What do you mean?"

"Maybe…
I mean,
have YOU thought
about telling
everyone?"

"Umm, not really?"

"Why not?"

"I'm not ready."

"That's okay,
but it might be
good,
you know?"

"I'll think
about it."

It's a Friday,
and I don't talk
to Levi for a few days.

Why
        would he think
        that I'm ready?

Why
        would he push
        me like this?

I'm not ready,
        I'm not ready,
                I'm not ready.

Right?

I liked the sureness
    of my life.
    Was okay,
    I thought.
    But I'm still living
    a secret.

What if
    my parents
    don't want me?
    Leave me like
    Nora's mom left her?

What if
    I was alone?

Where would I go?

Who would I be
    if I was nothing
    to them?

And Levi doesn't even know
    about the binding.

I don't even know
    if it's temporary
    or if this is what I'll do
    forever.

I'd have to buy
    a real binder.
    Because what I'm doing
    isn't good for me,
    can have real effects
    on my health,
    like hurting my spine
    or messing up my breathing.

    But

how can I do that
    without someone knowing?
    And

how can I do that
    without them thinking
    I'm a freak?

It's night,
     of course,
        when I wonder if
        Levi's awake still.

Maybe he even knows
        that I'm upset with him.

But I don't want to
        tell him this.
        Don't want to feel
        this pressure.

Don't want to be
        embarrassed of
        the pressure on my chest.

And

I'm not ready.

THE TALK

I'm eating breakfast when
    Mom asks:

                "Are you dating
                Levi?
                Is that why you spend
                so much time
                together?"

I nearly spit
    out my toast,
    "No, Mom,
    that's definitely not it."

                "Do you want to?"

"Date Levi?"

                "Yes. That's perfectly normal."

Oh, Mother.

"No, he's just
my best friend."

                    "Okay."

"Okay."

                    "I'm here if…"

"Mom."

                    "Have a nice day, Jamie."

My parents never had
        "the talk"
        with me.

And they don't know
        Levi's gay.

But they are good friends
        with his parents,
        so I can't trust them
        not to share his secret.

We never talk about romance.
        And as I drive to school,
        listening to another
        radio commercial
        about car insurance,

I realize that
        it was probably hard
        for her to ask.
        I was a normal teen
        (for once),

and maybe she's trying.
        And maybe she'd be okay
        one day.

Maybe.

Levi corners me
        as I wait in line
        for a muffin before
        first period.

He's never been afraid
        to have hard talks
        with me, so
        I knew
        this was coming.

Even though I didn't
        expect to *talk talk*
        at 7:30 a.m.

NOT THE SORT TO STAY MAD AT

Levi says,
        "You're mad at me."

I shrug.

"I guess I didn't like
how you responded."

            "I didn't mean
            to pressure you."

"Well…"

            "I'm sorry, J.
                You should
                take your time."

I soften.
"It's okay, Lev.
I'm just not ready,
okay?"

            "Absolutely."
              He pays
              for my muffin
              and

              before everyone else
              arrives, he adds,

"I'm thinking of
telling my parents."

"Oh?"

"Yeah, Evan's thinking
the same thing."
He looks down,
        peels the orange
            he'd bought for himself.

"We've been talking
about it for a while."

"You know
I support you."

"I'm thinking of
telling them tonight."

I breathe,
feel the air move
down and in,
past my binder.
(I can always feel it.)
And then
up and out.
"Wow."

                    "Yeah."
                        He finishes peeling,
                        pops a wedge
                        into his mouth. Says,
                    "Jason said I could
                        stay with him, if…"

"Do you think…?"

                    He shrugs,
                        his shoulders shifting
                        the weight of the world.
                    "I don't know,
                        honestly."

"What will you do,
just go to Jason's?"

        "I wrote myself
        a letter. Promising
        that I wouldn't
        hide if
        Mom and Dad wanted me to."

I smile,
      reach for
      his shoulder.
"And Evan?"

        "Eric offered him
        the same deal.
        Both of them being
        on the swim team helped."

He laughs.
"I don't think this
is what my dad meant
when he said
to be a
'guys' guy.'"

"It's all his fault."

"Oh yes, definitely."

It's crazy,
this feeling of
sending Levi off
to do something
I can't. And

I hope that
I'll joke like he does
when I do.

FRIENDS JUST WANT TO HAVE FUN

A stress ball lands
    between us.
        Jason catches it
        when Levi returns
        the volley.

Our friends have arrived,
    just as I get settled
    at our table. I
peel an orange, then hear:

            "What's up, y'all?"
            Eric grabs a wedge of orange. Says,
            "Jamie, I feel like
                it's been ages."

"Sorry, it's been
so long."

"Nah, it's okay."
     Eric's the most
     laid-back of us.
     Even though
     his parents put
     the most pressure
     on him.
          "We've all got
          stuff going on."

"Like that paper for
     Mr. Evenhouse?"
     Jason throws
     the stress ball up.
     Then fixes
     his backpack strap
     before catching the ball.

"That was brutal,
     I don't think
     I'll ever forget
     how to spell
     'guillotine'
     after that."

"Eight pages on
the French Revolution
was seven pages too many,"
Nora agrees.
"I never thought
I'd miss government."

"Anyway," says Callie,
(who's taking AP Euro History,
far scarier than our class),
"Can we all go
see a movie this weekend?"

I quickly agree,
"That'd be great."

"You and Levi
      aren't running off
      to something?"
            Jason asks,
            kind of harshly.

"Jamie is my beard
when I'm out
with Evan,"
            Levi says, ignoring
            Jason's tone.

I'm not sure
who's covering
for whom.

"A movie sounds great,"
Nora says.
"I already set a playdate
for the twins
with some neighborhood
kids."

Nora looks thrilled,
a night off
from mothering her brothers.

Eric says,
"Just give me time
to nap after practice
in the morning, and
I'm all set to go."
Poor Eric, having to sport.

I don't tell him
that I'd cry if
I had to rise with the sun
to go swimming. Thinking,
Binders can't even go
in the water.

"Okay, Saturday at six, then?"
Callie settles this.
"Speaking of time,
I'm off to class."

We split into pairs,
Eric and Callie to English,
Jason and Nora to Spanish,
and Levi and I to chemistry.

"My mom asked if
we were dating,"
I say.

"What'd you say?"
Levi asks.

"That that's not the case."

"Does she think...?"
He looks at me,
and nearly bumps
into the guy in front of him,
forgetting high school
hallway traffic
for a moment.

"She's got no clue."
I roll my eyes,
"I don't even think
she believed me,
to be honest."

"That's good," he says.

"Can't spill the beans early."

"It'll be okay, Lev."

"Let's not talk
            about it anymore,
            okay?"

"Sure,
but
let me know
if you change your mind?
And what happens?"

"Of course."
            He reaches down,
            squeezes my hand
            in the crowded hall.
                        "Thanks, J."

CAN YOU HEAR ME BREATHING?

"My Dad's bowling later.
Want to come over?"
Nora asks
while we run
the mile in gym.
"It's been so long
since we hung out.
We could watch a movie
and do homework?"

"Sure,"
        I agree,
        not wanting to add
        to the idea that
        I prefer Levi to
        everyone else.

        (Right now,
        though,
        I do).

"Great!
The twins will be happy
to see you!"
        Her face lights up,
        and I feel guilty that
        I haven't told her.
    (And that I'm still not going to.)

"Just let me know
when he's gone, and
I'll come over."

            "That's perfect.
                Thanks
                    for understanding."

We stop talking
after that because we've got a 10-minute limit
or else we have to run it again.
Something about state standards,
I guess.

The binder makes this
harder. And
I become aware
of how loudly
I'm breathing.

Can everyone hear me?
The up and down
of my chest.
The in and out
of air.

Sometimes,
people comment on
how loudly I breathe.
And that means they know
that there's something
different
          about me.

Never, though,
would they be able to guess.

Nora keeps pace
        with me, even though
        I think she's faster.
        And
        it would be nice
        to tell her. To ask her
        if I breathe loudly.
        To have her
        help me
        cover it
        with chitchat.

But Nora,
        Nora has enough—
        her father,
        her brothers.
She doesn't need to
        worry about me,
        too.

OTHER PEOPLE HAVE PROBLEMS, TOO

Later that night,
    I park
    on the street,
    then shoulder
        my backpack.

        Nora's already texted
          to say,
                "Dad's gone."
So I don't knock,
just walk in
like I have
since I was a kid.
Before Connor and Colin
      were born.
Before Nora's
      dad's drinking.

"Jamie!"

                         "Jamie!"

Connor and Colin barrel
    through when they hear
    the door open.
        Little

              cartoons
                    running.

(I can't even see which feet
              belong to which boy.)

"Hey, boyos!"
    I say.
    They laugh at
    their nickname.
"What are we watching?"

    I don't catch
    the name of
    the cartoon movie

    but I follow

        them into the

           living room.

"Do you mind
watching this?"
Nora asks shyly.
"It's the easiest
way to keep them
occupied."

"Of course not!"
I quickly reply,
h e f t i n g
my backpack
down
onto the nearest sofa.

I follow it,
crossing my legs
on her carpet.
Using cushions as a desk.

"Definitely don't want to
do this trig homework."

"Oh, you and me both, J."

Nora and I used to
        spend hours
                in her home.

        Her dad taught me
                how to do
                        my multiples of nine
                        on my hands:

                        "If you want to do
                                two times nine—

"That's eighteen, Mr. Richards."

                        He laughed,
                        "Well, yes, but
                        if you put your
                        second finger down,
                                the tens come before
                                        the space,
                                and the ones after it."

"So...I have one before
        and
                eight after."

                        "Which is eighteen!"

"Eighteen!"

Mr. Richards started
        drinking a few years
            ago

(right after the twins
were born),

                    and Nora's never said
                    why.

        It's nice to be here,

                    to listen
                    to Connor and Colin.

        Because Nora will say
            anything

                        so she can feel like
                        her life is

                            normal.

And, tonight, it's nice to be
the one supporting,
        rather than
        the one needing
        support.

I keep my phone
next to me in case
Levi needs anything.

"What's been happening
in your life?"
Nora asks, sitting
in the corner
of the couch,
knees up as a desk
while she works.

"Not much,"
I lie.
"Steve's coming home
to visit this weekend."

"That'll be fun!"

"Yeah!
It'll be nice to see him."

"I haven't seen him
in ages."

"Since before he left
for college?"

"Yeah, he was always
so fun when we were
kiddos."

"I'll tell him you say
hi.'"

SECRETS TAKE UP SO MUCH SPACE

The thing about Nora
    is that
    she's such a
    gossip.

She's so
    sweet
    and
    caring

that people tell
    her
    everything.
    So she
    (always)
    knows what's
    going on.

We update each other
    on what
    we've heard:
    Johnny's doing *that*,
    Miguel's going to college *there*,
    and Sofie's dating *her*.

It's not that
        we really care
        or will share
        secrets outside
        of our friends.

We just like to know.
        But it tastes
        funny tonight.

This is the first
        time I've had
        my own
        gossip-worthy
        secret. So I say,

"Can we not talk
        about this stuff?"

                                "Oh." Nora's surprised.
                                "Sure,
                                        is everything okay?"

"Yeah, I just
        don't feel like it."

Not too much later,
        Nora's dad calls
        and says to
        warm up
        dinner. So

I leave.

When I get home,
        I text Nora
        from the car
        and thank her.
        Promise that
        everything is good
        between us and that
        I hope her dad
        wasn't too hard on her.

I still haven't heard
        from Levi,
        so I send a
        "<3"

My *Ghostbusters* ringtone sounds.

It's past midnight,
         but I always sleep
         with my phone on loud.

"Hello?"

                              "J!"

"Lev?"
         I sit up.
         "Oh my God,
         Lev!"

                              "It went well!"
                                       He answers before
                                       I can even ask.

"They were okay?"

                              "Yes! I'm still crying,
                                       I'm so happy."

"What happened?"

                              "Jamie, it was so good.
                                       They said
                                       they loved me
                                       and they want me
                                       no matter what.
                                       That this
                                       doesn't change *anything*."

"And Evan?"
Levi pauses.
There's a shift here,
like he feels he can't
be happy anymore.
"He's at Eric's.
His parents
don't want him
around his sister."

I don't say
that this
scares me,

that I stop
breathing
for a second.

Because what if
what if
what if
this is what happens to me?

I say,
"Levi…
I'm so sorry."

Like I'm also
apologizing
to myself.

Then, there's not much to say, so I add:

"Maybe you should
get some sleep?"

      "Yeah, you're right."
       I listen to him yawn.

I try to do
the same thing.

Evan is
   sweet,
   kind,
   scared,
   lost, and
   at Eric's.

I dream of
   being him.
   I wake up
   sweating,
   afraid that

I saw the future.

AT THE MOVIES

It takes us too long
        to figure out
        whose turn it is
        to pick the movie.

And we're all quiet
        as we try to explain
        why we haven't
        seen each other
        so much.

Like it's a secret
        we're keeping
        from one another.

(Of course, for me,
        it is.)

"Levi just came out to
      his parents.
      He should choose the movie."
                  Jason asserts this like
                  Fred in *Scooby-Doo*
                  saying,
                  "Well, gang,
                  let's split up and
                  search for clues."

      "Yeah, you're right,"
            says Callie. And
            we all agree.

Will they celebrate me
      like this?

Or will I be like Evan,
      whose situation
      we don't talk about,

too sad to celebrate?

We each buy tickets.
> Then Jason and I collect
> > money for snacks.
> Eric and Callie go
> > to get seats.
> > (Callie will pick the best ones.
> > And Eric is confident enough
> > to save them.) And
> Nora and Levi always
> > go to the bathroom
> > before a movie.

It's always fun
> to see our routine
> in action.
> Our little family.

When the lights come up,
    I stand and stretch
    between Nora and Levi.
    We compare notes
        on the movie.

           "Guys, my feet are asleep!"
           Eric whines.
           (This, too, is routine.)
           And Callie kicks him.
           (So is that.)

We file out to the parking lot
    and part for the weekend.
    Eric, Jason, and Callie
        each have practice tomorrow.
    Nora's got the twins.
    Levi's out with Evan.
    I'm hiding out
        to write a paper.

           We promise not to go
               so long that we forget
               again.

Levi and I carpooled.
He looks at me.
"I see you, J.
What're you thinking about?"

"I miss them."

"Me too.
Do you think Evan
fits in?"

"Yeah,"
I agree quietly,
hoping that
my coming out
is as well-received.
"We all love him..."

"I'm going to bring him
more when we're
with everyone. I think…"
Levi pauses, and I see his
guilt for being accepted by
his family when Evan isn't.

"I think he could use it.
Some more people
on his side,
I mean."

"He's got us.
It's going to be okay."

I go home and
try to be as confident as I sound.

132

STEVE COMES HOME

A few years ago,
  Steve used to
  drive home from college
  in just enough time
  to pick me up
  from school.

He'd yell
  for me
  as I tried
  to get on
  the bus

because he knew
  I'd forget
  which day
  he was coming home.

Now,
  he still tries
  to surprise me,
  even though I drive myself.

Except
  he's usually
  not very good
  at it.

Today,
    he catches me
        on the stairs. He springs
        from the closet
        underneath them.

I nearly fall
    down. Then, laughing, I
    hug him. And he comes

upstairs with me
    to chat.

And then,
    we're sitting
    on the bed when
    he notices:

        "Is that my old
           Beatles shirt?"

He tugs on my sleeve,
    shows taped straps,
      asks,

        "Jamie, why is there
        tape on something
        under this?"

Oh crap.

My first thought is to say
        it's "a girl thing."
    But not only
    is it a lie,
    it's so...*gender*-filled.

So I
        fix my shirt.
    Pull it back into place.
    Try to
            stop
            the panicked
            beatbeatbeatbeatbeat
            of my heart.

            Breathe.
            Please, just breathe.

                                "Jamie, it's okay.
                                    Whatever it is,
                                    it's okay."

And I remember
        how well
        Steve knows me.

"You're panicking.
            Don't—it's okay."

"Have you heard
      of people
   who bind their chest?"

      I prepare to explain.

            "Yes."

I pause. "What?"
            "I have a friend
                  who is transgender.
               He binds his chest
                     to look more
                     like a guy."

"Oh."

            "Is that what—"
               Steve motions to me,
                     "that's for?"

"Yeah…"
      I shrug.

"There are better ways,
　　　I know.
　　　But how could I tell
　　　Mom and Dad?"

　　　　　　　　　"This isn't good for you,
　　　　　　　　　　　Jame."
　　　　　　　　　The mention of
　　　　　　　　　my nickname
　　　　　　　　　makes me feel
　　　　　　　　　worse.
　　　　　　　　　"I mean, binding's
　　　　　　　　　　　totally okay."

"What?"
　　　I look up
　　　　　　from the floor
　　　　　　for the first time
　　　　　　in what feels like
　　　　　　　　　h o u r s.
"You're not
　　　disappointed?"

　　　　　　　　　"Oh no, kiddo."
　　　　　　　　　Steve leans against
　　　　　　　　　　　my bed.
　　　　　　　　　"You do you.
　　　　　　　　　　　I'm kind of
　　　　　　　　　　　　　curious about
　　　　　　　　　　　　　why you do it.
　　　　　　　　　But it's okay
　　　　　　　　　　　as long as
　　　　　　　　　　　you're doing it
　　　　　　　　　safely."

137

I look at Steve,
        drop my jaw,
        catch some flies,
        blink.
(Every cliché
        about being
        surprised
        becomes real.)

So, of course,
        thinking he
        might be
        okay,
        I risk it:

"I'm genderqueer."

                        "Cool."

"Yeah?"

                        "Of course,
                                Jamie.
                        Do you want
                                to talk more about it?"

So I tell him
        everything.
        And suddenly, Levi's not
                the only one to
                        know.

WHY I KEEP MY OLDER BROTHER AROUND

My mom knocks
    20 minutes
    later.
She's happy, I think,
that Steve and I
    are so close.

        "Steve, honey,
           where do you
                want to go
          for dinner?"

        "Ah,"

              he says.
              Pauses.
              Thinks.

        Then,
        (finally)
        so as to keep her out,
           replies,
        "Something with tacos?"

           She accepts this. Says,
        "Oh, there's this
           great place that just
           opened…"

She keeps talking,
        then her voice fades
                down the stairs.

                        "I'm assuming
                        Mom and Dad
                        don't know?"
                                Steve asks.
"No, and
        I don't want them to
        right now.

I don't even know
        how to
        explain
        it."

                "Okay,
                        take your time.
                                I do think
                                        that they'll be
                                        alright with it,
                                                if
                                                that
                                                helps."

"It does.
Thanks,
Steve."

I'm tired,
  and I think
  that we're done.
  Then Steve says:

      "I'm gonna be here
        for about a
          week.
      Why don't I
        order
        a real binder
        for you?

      They won't see
        the charge.

      Won't open
        packages
        for me…"

"…won't know."

      "Exactly.
        They won't know.

"Steve…
  would you mind?

That would make
  my life
  so much
  better."

      "Of course.
        Just email me
          a link tonight."

"I'll make sure it gets here
before I leave."

I get up
        and hug Steve.
        I cry
                (finally).

                "I have your back,
                        kiddo."
                He rests
                        his head
                                on mine.
                "Just always
                        remember:
                        you're everything
                                you need to be
                                right now
                                and
                                it's enough."

I am everything I need to be right now and it's enough.

Steve goes downstairs.
        Plays his role as
        the visiting child.

And I sink
        into
                my bed
        and breathe.

Going from fear
        to validation
                        to fear
                                to acceptance

        in such a short
        time

drained me.
                But
                Steve was okay.

At least one
        person
        in my family
                is okay with it
                                (with me).

I grab my phone
         to tell Levi.
         Happy to keep up
         the streak
                  of happy coming-outs.

"Steve knows!"
(I text.)

                                   "An '!' means
                                   it's OK,
                                   right?"
                                   (Levi answers.)

"Yes!

He was so nice
         about it!

He said
         he has a trans friend
         that uses
         different pronouns
         that I could
         talk to
         about gender stuff!"

                                   "J, that's awesome!"

"I feel so good
         about it!"

                          "Yes!
                                   It's such a
                                            good feeling."

144

SOMETIMES MY MOM MAKES ME
WANT TO JUMP OUT OF A MOVING VEHICLE

My mom likes
      to surprise me
      in the car.

Our large SUV
      in which
      I learned to drive.

(Though I have
      my own,
      much smaller,
      car named Chip).

I think it's because
      she knows
      I can't escape.

When my grandparents
        got a divorce,
        she told me
        on the
        ride home
                from the bookstore.

When she was laid off (for two, too-long months)
        just before
                I started
                high school,
        she told me
        after treating me
                to ice cream.

Tonight,
        we're riding
        home
                from the mall.
        (I needed
        new jeans.)

"So I ran into
Evan Holmes'
mother at the store
yesterday."

It's impressive
how her eyes
never leave the road
but she still seems
able to *look*
at me.

I brace myself.

"Oh?"

"She said he's dating Levi!"

"Yeah…"

"I didn't know he was
gay."

"Does it matter?"

I don't want this
          to be
          an important talk.
But I can feel myself
          putting weight
          on her reaction,
as if it will
          predict my future.

                    "I mean, no.
                         It's different.
                    But I thought you and he…"

"Why's it different?"
          I look at
          the lines on my hand
          like a palm reader.

What will my future be?

"We just don't have
a lot of
people who are gay
in our town."
She huffs.
"Jamie, I didn't bring this up
to be criticized."

"Why'd you
bring it up?"

What was it that Steve told me to remember?

"Because I thought
you and Levi
were dating."

"We aren't."
I shrug.
And she does it again—
eyes on the road
but looking at me.

Oh, yeah. I am everything I need to be right now and it's enough.

"Why'd you let me
think you were?"

"I didn't mean to."
I didn't stop it,
since she kept
bringing it up.

I am everything I need to be right now and it's enough.

"Okay. Just…
          sometimes I feel like
          you're lying to me,
          Jamie. And I don't
          want that."

"I'm not lying
          to you, Mom."

          She nods,
               "I was sorry
               to hear
               Evan was kicked out.
               And I told Mrs. Holmes so."

MY MOM HAS MORE PROS THAN CONS

I grab
>the bag of new jeans,
>thank my mother,
>and hurry inside
>>to overthink
>>and panic.

Why did it seem
>like she was hiding
>>her thoughts?

Why does it matter
>that we don't have
>a lot of people
>who are gay
>in our town?

Why does she seem
>disappointed
>that Levi isn't
>my boyfriend?

At least,
 I think,
she said she was sorry to hear about Evan.

And from there,
 flows a list of positives:

She didn't say
 it was bad
 to be gay.

She didn't say
 anything mean
 about
 my best friend.

She didn't say,

                              "Jamie, you better not
                                    be different."
She didn't see
 the secret
 in my head. And

she wants
 the truth,
 so she can't be mad
 when (if) I tell her.

These are all good things.

I repeat again:

I am everything I need to be right now and it's enough.

WHEN THE TRUTH BANGS AT THE DOOR

The subject of Levi and Evan
      comes up
      at dinner
      the next night.

Steve's still here,
      and we're sitting
      in our dining room.

That's unusual
      in general,
      but when Steve's here,
      we do a lot of family things.

                "Oh, that's great,"
                   Steve says,
                   when mom announces
                   Levi's relationship.
                   "Good for them.
                   It takes a lot of
                       courage to
                       come out."

I smile and say,
      "They're really happy
      that they did."
      Like I'm just talking about
         the boys.

             "Yes, it does,"
               my father says.

"My college roommate
         didn't come out
         until much later,"
Steve says.

"When Charlie came out
         as trans,
         it was really rough
         with his family."
My brother is untouchable,
         and he knows it,
         so he adds,
"Which I think is unfair."

"Trans?"
Mom asks.

"Transgender,"
      I manage to say,
      much more carefully.

Steve says,
         "Charlie was born
         as a female biologically,
         but he identifies as male."

      "Interesting…"
            Mom says.

She doesn't seem too
pleased.
         Spears a tomato
         in her salad,
               changes
               the subject.

Steve stops by
        my room later
        after everyone else
        goes to bed.

                                "Hey, kiddo."

"Hey, kidbro."

                                "How are you
                                        doing?
                                Dinner was…
                                        interesting."

It doesn't help
        that he says
                "interesting"
        like she did,
        even though
        he probably
                doesn't realize.

"What if Mom
        hates me?"

                                "Mom's not going
                                        to hate you."

"Steve…
        you saw her
        tonight."

                                "She adores you.
                                She brags about you,
                                tells me that you're great."

"Steve."
    I repeat,
        frustrated.
    I'm allowed to feel this,
        to fear that.

            "I know it's scary."

                He breathes,
                "Okay, it's not
                    something
                    I've had to
                    think
                    about.
                But the thought
                  of coming out
                  scares me,
                so I can only imagine
                what you're feeling.

                That also means
                    I'm so proud."

"I'm scared."

            "It's okay to be scared."
            Steve rubs my back.
            And I let him.
                "It's okay."

I'M TIRED OF SECRETS

It feels heavier
    now,

holding this
    secret.

At school, I
    wonder

how long it will be like
    this—

Where I feel like a
    liar
        a
    coward
        a
    fraud—

when I'm none of those,
    right?

"Lev,"
        I say.
        I catch him
                after school.
"I'm freaking out."

        Levi looks at me
        And I think he sees
                the duct tape
                        holding in tears.
                The toothpicks
                        holding up smiles.
                The calm
                        that is the storm.

                "Okay, J,
                        let's go."

                                He finds Evan,
                                        picking his
                                        boyfriend out
                                        of the crowd
                                        without
                                        having to
                                        search for
                                        his red hair.

                                Telling him
                                that he can't
                                go for coffee
                                right now.

Levi drives.

My teeth
    shake in the cold.

My fingers
    shake in the panic.
        The fear
            finally allowed
            out
            even when the secret is not.

My brain is
    relieved,
        letting go of its hold
            on the false face
            beaten by fear.

                Levi looks concerned,
                        pulling into
                        an empty
            parking lot. "Talk to me, J."

"I think my mom
    will hate me."

                "That's not going
                    to happen."

My brain screams
out about
her reaction to his
coming out.

But even now,
(even like this)
I can't tell him.
Another secret to keep.

"Jamie,
I need you
to

b r e a t h e

for me."

B r e a t h e.

"No matter what,
Steve has your back,
and so do I."

He whispers,

"Your family isn't Evan's."

I close my eyes.

I am everything I need to be right now and it's enough.

"I hate this.
　　Nothing is happening,
　　　　and I'm a mess."

　　　　　　Levi laughs,
　　　　　　　"*A lot* is
　　　　　　　　　happening.
　　　　　　　You always get
　　　　　　　annoyed
　　　　　　　when you have a
　　　　　　　　panic attack.

　　　　　　But, J,
　　　　　　　you're
　　　　　　　allowed to
　　　　　　　　panic."

161

"It was so good
        to figure myself
        out,
        to know who I am.

But the fact that
        I feel like
                I'm lying
                to everyone

        makes me feel
                like garbage.

And I can't change
        that I am
                who I am.

But I can change
        that it's a secret.

But I can't control
        the hate people
        may have
for what I am."

Then,
in this car,
  heat finally kicking in,

  Levi tells me,

      "It's okay
      to keep secrets,

      but it's better
      to be yourself."

He remembers.

      "Fear tells you
      you're these things.

      You're not
      doing anything

      wrong."

          He smiles.

              "For once, Jamie,
              let it be about you.

              Tell them
              when you feel
              like you're ready,
              not when you feel
              like they are."

"THE DAY"

I let weeks
        go by.

            And I am myself

                    for myself.

I get to know
        genderqueer Jamie.

The binder Steve buys me
        is great.
                Black and much more
                  comfortable.

            Less noticeable if you're looking,
               invisible if you aren't.

I feel good.
I still don't have a plan,
no day feels like The Day
to tell them, but then…

My parents are watching
        the news, and
        there's a kid
        who is trans.

                        "I don't understand," Mom says.
                        "How could that little girl know?"

                        "I'm not sure," my father agrees.
                        "It's not a genetic thing."
                        Like he would know. Because he's
                        a scientist.

Is this how
        they would talk
        about me?
I'm so surprised that now,
        I have to know.

"It doesn't matter
how old you are," I blurt out.

My dad notices
        me shaking, pauses
        the news.

Then I say,
"I need you to support me."

                        They say "of course"
                        quickly, looking panicked,
                        looking surprised.

Here goes:
"I'm genderqueer."

I breathe
    deeply,
    thankful, proud even, that
    it (I) came out
    without fear.

        There's a long pause.

          "Okay, honey,"
          says my father,
          slowly.
          "I think I know what
          that means. But
          can you explain
          so I'm sure?"

I think
    he may be
    lying.

But I also think
    he's doing it
    to make me
    feel okay.

So I explain.

A LITTLE DOES GO A LONG WAY

My parents
      don't really
      understand
      what I am.

But my parents
      understand
      who I am.
      That their kiddo
      is still everything
      that they wanted me to be.

                  ("Maybe more,"
                      my Dad adds,
                      hugging me.)

I'm able to sink safely
      in their arms.
      And I let fear
            turn into tears of gratitude
                  and relief.

It takes some time
        for my parents to turn
                "she" into "they,"

        "daughter" into "child" or "kiddo."
                (Or "spawn" which is what Dad
                has always joked about anyway.)

        "Gender" into a spectrum.
                Going from
                        two defined things
                into something
                        much bigger.

Steve,
        of course,
                answers questions
                they're afraid to ask me

        (mostly about grandchildren).

Mom is slow,
	hates being corrected,
	but she is trying.
		A sigh turns
			into a
			question of

				"How can I do this better?"

Dad learns
	too quickly,
	and I have to tell him
	not to be
"too embarrassing,"

			that

"I still hate attention, Dad"

		when he tries to
		single-handedly
		defeat
		the gender binary.

I'VE NEVER BEEN HAPPIER TO BE WRONG

Levi smiles
     his goofy grin
     when I tell him
     at school.
     Lifts me up,
          laughing.
          Saying, "I told you so"
          over and over again.

And while I'd normally
     be mad at him
     for rubbing it in,

I grin and say,
"You were right.
You were right.
You were right, Lev."

I tell him
        that I want to
        get used to my parents
        knowing

("It's still crazy
        that they know!")

        before I tell
        our friends.

It's not me
        hiding from them.

("Okay, maybe it's me
        hiding a little bit.")

But there are so many
        feelings
        that come with
        coming out.

And this way,
     my parents
     can adapt.

So they don't say
     anything
     offensive
     in front of
     everyone.

But I will, soon.
     I want to soon.

I'm excited for them
     to know me, too.

DOWN BY THE WATER

It's November,
      and we're given
      one more warm weekend.
      A surprise bookended by
      cold fronts. So

it only seems right
      to slip down to
      the water.

Everyone has said that
      I seem different.
      But, of course,
      only Levi knows why.

So, sitting there,
      skipping rocks,

I break our rules.
      I make no announcement
      of a secret.

I say,

"Hey,
        I use they/them pronouns now."

I don't cry or
        let them ask
        any questions.

And it's funny
        to think I was afraid,
        but I know it's normal.

I know I'm normal.
        Well,
        at least,
        this isn't what
        makes me weird...

but my friends knew that
        already.

Jason asks questions.
      Eric gets protective.
      Callie stays quiet.
      Nora smiles as if she knew.
      Levi makes a joke.

Then,
      we go back to
      what we were doing.

Someone suggests
      we order a pizza,
      and we laugh
      at the idea of
      an unlucky delivery person
         climbing
         down here.

                "I don't think we'd
                   ever have enough
                   money to tip them
                   for that," Jason says.

CATCHING "IT"

The sound of
    a ball in a glove.

The *thwack*,
        a knock
        announcing
        its arrival.

The pinch
    of the glove
    covered by my hand,
    so the ball doesn't fall
        out.

And the decision of
    how to throw
    a secret
    so it leaves
    my hand
        just right.

These things have always
    made me feel
    in control.

So I always ask Steve
    to play catch
    when he comes home.

One of my grandmas
        has decided to
        decide what I am
        (a freak).

And one of our aunts
        has decided to
        agree with her.

        And also
        to not speak
        to me.

Even when I think
        that the ball
                has a better chance
                of hitting me
        than of me
                catching it,

I still try. So I wonder
        why I learned that
        and they didn't.

It's a better use
        of time than
        when I cry
        and wonder
        what's wrong with me
        that they don't
        love me anymore.

I wish I could tell them, with a smile:
        queer isn't contagious.

My parents
        do what
        they think
        is best and

        try to
        shield me
        from a world
        that I've
        always
        known.

Where
gender
                is
                everywhere.
And so

I play
the adult
and

take the
fear

others have
of me
                and
                        I am stronger

(in the moment).

                I let it take
                        its toll later. Then
                                let it go.

I wouldn't say
         it's easy
         knowing that

some people
         would demand
         a gender. And that

my driver's license
         will still say
         "F" where

other states
         allow an
         "X." Or that

so many places
         make me choose
         a restroom based on signs.

Gender is still everywhere,
         the most popular pair
         since black and white.

And why must I say that
     "I'm lucky"
     to be accepted
     rather than to say,
     "People need to do better.
     I'm still a person"?

It's easy to be angry.
     But then it's harder to
     be okay
     (even if I'm right)
     because being mad
     is so
     t i r i n g.

(I spent some time practicing
     this anger, and sometimes,
     I still do.)

THE SECOND READING

When I talk about
      the reading,
      it's Nora who
      falls in love
      with the image

of a poet
      speaking
      in a small space.

Of seeing art
      up close,

having never been able to go.
      So Levi watches the twins,
      and I promise she'll be home
      soon.

Selfishly, I find
　　　　another queer poet,
　　　　and they too
　　　　speak so casually
　　　　about binding.

Nora leans over,
　　　　whispers questions
　　　　about it, so

without thinking, I say,
　　　　"Yeah,
　　　　it's really common
　　　　in the community.
　　　　I do it, too."

She nods. Says,
　　　　"Thanks, Jamie."

I get home later,
      slide
      another book of poetry
      next to the first.

I drop into
      the chair,
      panic.

Feel my heart race
      behind my eyes,
      in my chest,
      on my wrists.

Almost text Nora,
      beg her to keep
      this secret. And

then,
      I breathe,
      repeat,
            "It's really common."

I check for feelings
     of shame,
     of fear,
     of regret,

thinking they couldn't
     have passed
     for good. But

for now, at least,
     they're gone,
     and I smile.

I still won't
    tell my parents
    right now.

But that door
    doesn't seem
    shut so tightly.

And I think
    I trust them
        when they say
        "I love you" now.

So "The Day" exists again,
    except it'll just be
    "a day" in my future,
    I hope.

EVERYONE HAS A SECRET IN HIGH SCHOOL

At least, that's what
    my older brother, Steve, says,

    and he's right.

Some girls date boys.
    And even these girls
    sometimes keep this
    from their parents.
    Parents who judge
    boyfriends based
    on race, money,
    things we can't control.

Some girls ask:
    "Hey Mom, Dad,
    can I have a friend
    over to watch Disney movies?"
    But that girl-space-friend isn't
    just a "friend."
    But their parents
    would never say "okay"
    if they knew that.

Some girls play
             spin the bottle,
             around and around it goes,
             but I still don't know.

My friends see movies
and eat ice cream,
             and, according to my mother,
             we're growing.

(I think
she's proud
that we can
talk about
certain things
in a way
she never could.)

I'm pretty sure now
             my parents
             would never believe
             that I was one of
             "those girls."

Because I'm not.

We have secrets too,
but not all of them
are the same as they
used to be.

    Levi's gay.
        (He and Evan Holmes
        won Homecoming Court
        this year, and
        Levi's parents were proud of both of them.)

    Nora's dad still drinks too much.
        (She's thinking about telling
        someone though.)

    Eric dropped out of swimming.
        And his mother has
        finally accepted it.

    Jason and Callie
        tell us
                she's not sure she's straight and
                he feels like he doesn't have a secret.
                (We say "that's okay" to both.)

We still pile into Eric's van,
and drive to the park.

Climb down
onto the rocks
by the canal.
Off of the trails where

our parents
brought us for
Sunday cookouts.
Days with
picture-perfect
picnic baskets, and
family Frisbee matches.

We talk about
    our classmates and
    our teachers.
    Complain about
    assignments, tests,
    and quizzes.

    We talk about
    everything. Including
    how good it is to
        be honest with each other.
    And how lucky we are
        to always return here.

One by one,
we have each come

to the canal,
picked a normal weekend outing.

Held court.
Called a meeting.
All of those adult terms.
And we realize that
we've all changed so much
because we've come
to say to the water
what scared us most.

We still keep secrets,
    and we still tell our own.

All of us.

But we don't let fear
    decide what's a secret
    and what isn't.

Because it is safety, rather than secrets,
    that binds us together.

WANT TO KEEP READING?

If you liked this book, check out another book
from West 44 Books:

SECOND IN COMMAND BY SANDI VAN

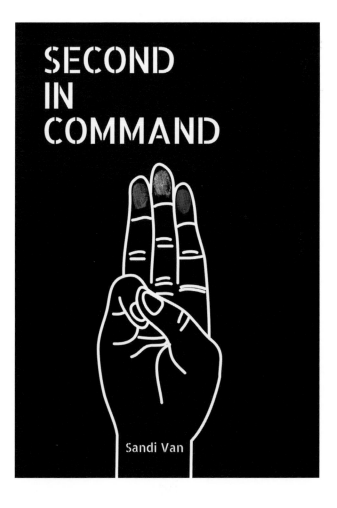

THE DAY MOM LEFT

Early in the morning—
so early
the darkness was a blanket
over my face.

Like when Jack and I
would build a fort in the family room,
hide underneath,
and eat bowls of salty popcorn.

You better clean up those crumbs,
Mom would say.

Today she says,
Goodbye.
I love you.
Take care of Reina,
and Daddy,
and each other.

Six months will go by fast,
I promise.

Then she kisses us each
three times—
once on the left cheek,
once on the right,
once on the forehead,
her lips like wet dough.

Check out more books at:
www.west44books.com

ABOUT THE AUTHOR

Rory James is a writer from Cleveland, Ohio. She holds degrees in creative writing, English, and political science. Rory now teaches test prep classes to high school students. Inspired by her own experience with gender issues, Rory hopes to reach the many young people with struggles or questions of their own.